# KINGS OF THE CASTLE

*For Lucy*

A TEMPLAR BOOK

First published in the UK in 2016 by Templar Publishing,
part of the Bonnier Publishing Group,
The Plaza, 535 King's Road, London, SW10 0SZ
www.templarco.co.uk
www.bonnierpublishing.com

1 3 5 7 9 10 8 6 4 2

ISBN 978-1-78370-258-9 (Hardback)
ISBN 978-1-78370-259-6 (Paperback)

Designed by Verity Clark
Edited by Katie Haworth

Printed in China

# KINGS OF THE CASTLE

Victoria Turnbull

templar publishing

George didn't want to waste
the night moonbathing.

He wanted to
build a sandcastle

that would turn
any monster

green eyed
with envy . . .

. . . but Boris had other ideas.

. . . came the strangest looking
creature George had ever seen.

George decided to introduce himself – the creature couldn't be worse company than Boris.

But

it

was

hopeless.

They

could

not

understand

one

another.

George thought it
was time to go . . .

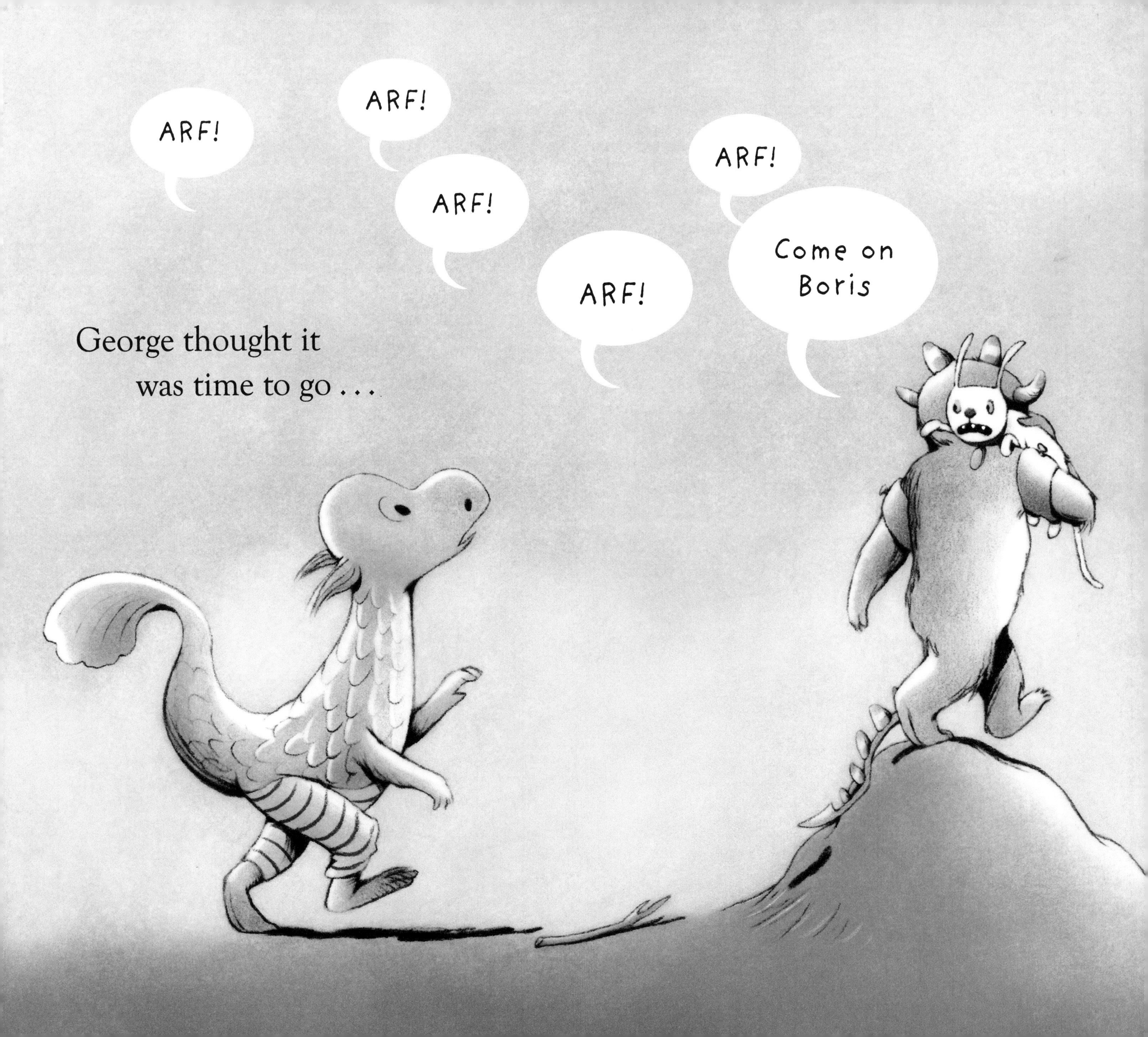

. . . but Boris had other ideas.

Boris!

Maybe they could be friends after all.

And so with a
little planning . . .

. . . George and Nepo set to work.

And before long, the flag
could be raised.

George and Nepo
had done it.
They were now . . .

They reigned until dawn.

When the tide came in and the sun came up,

they headed for home.

The night was over . . .

. . . but some things last forever.

Also by **Victoria Turnbull**

# THE
# SEA
# TIGER

*"I am the sea tiger.*
*I am Oscar's best friend.*
*Together, we travel to*
*EXTRAORDINARY PLACES*
*under a sea studded*
*with stars."*

RRP £12.99 – ISBN 978-1-78370-006-6 (HB)
RRP £7.99 – ISBN 978-1-78370-007-3 (PB)

*'. . . lyrical, elegiac and highly imaginative'* – winner of
the 2013 Association of Illustrators New Talent Award,
Children's Book category

**Victoria Turnbull** was born in York, and spent her childhood absorbed by books and drawing.

After studying Graphic Design at Staffordshire University, she went on to take up a place on the MA in Children's Book Illustration at the Cambridge School of Art, graduating in 2013.

As part of her MA, Victoria created a picture book, *The Sea Tiger,* which has seen her named the winner of the Association of Illustrators New Talent Award 2013 (Children's Book Category) and was published by Templar in June 2014. *The Sea Tiger* was also shortlisted for the Waterstones Children's Book Prize, 2015.

Victoria now lives in London, where she both writes and illustrates her own stories.

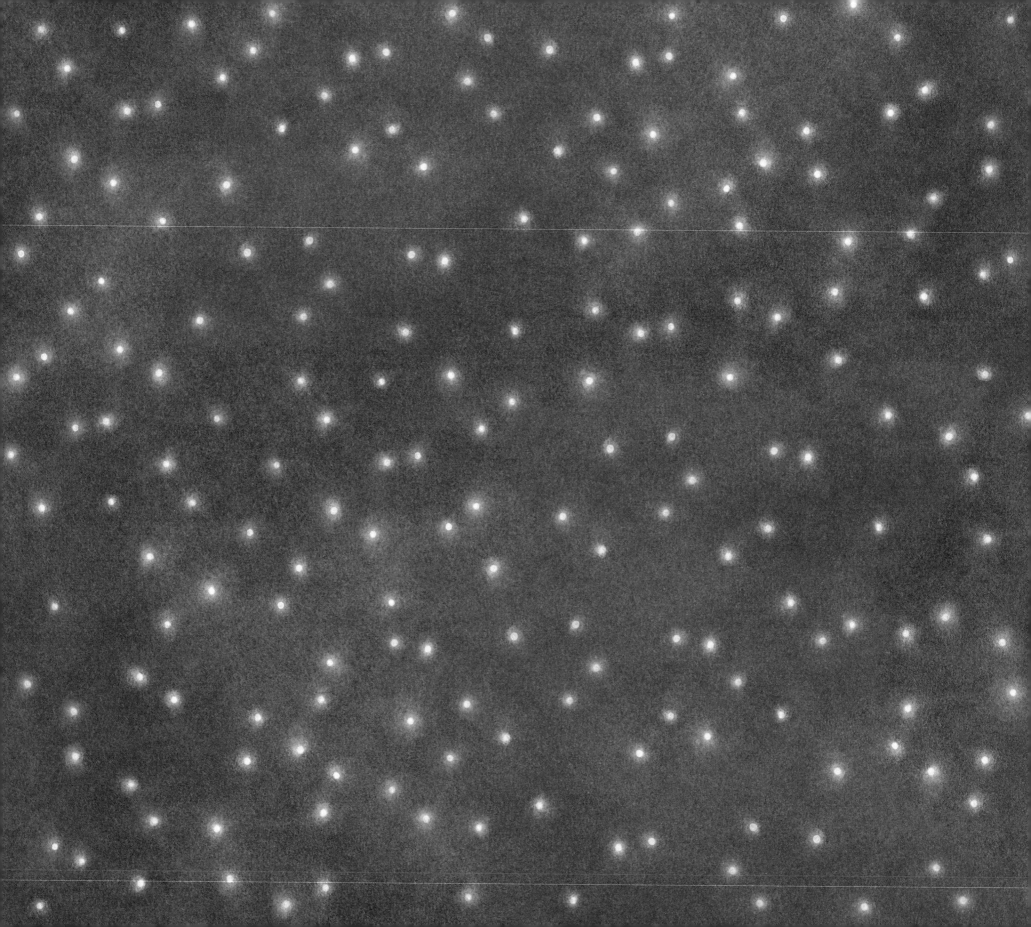